A BRIDE FOR CHRISTMAS

SPINSTER MAIL-ORDER BRIDES

(BOOK 2)

By

Cheryl Wright

Contents

A Bride for Christmas

(Spinster Mail-Order Brides – Book Two)

Copyright ©2019 by Cheryl Wright

Cover Artist: Black Widow Books

Thanks

Thanks to my very dear friends (and authors), Margaret Tanner and Susan Horsnell for their enduring encouragement.

Thanks also to Alan, my husband of over 44 years, who has been a relentless supporter of my writing for many years.

And last, but by no means least, I must thank all my wonderful readers who encourage me to continue writing these stories. It is such a joy to me, knowing so many of you enjoy reading my stories. I love writing them as much as you love reading them.

About the Author

Multi-published, best-selling and award-winning author, Cheryl Wright, former secretary, debt collector, account manager, writing coach, and shopping tour hostess, loves reading.

She writes both historical and contemporary western romance, as well as contemporary romance and romantic suspense.

She lives in Melbourne, Australia, and is married with two adult children and has six grandchildren.

When she's not writing, she can be found in her craft room making greeting cards.

Check out Cheryl's Amazon page for a full list of her other books.

Other Links:

http://cheryl-wright.com

https://www.facebook.com/cherylwrightauthor

Join my newsletter here!

Chapter One

Westlake, Wyoming 1879

Melody Harken started her day at 5.30am.

The temperature was brisk, it was coming on for winter, and she pulled her robe up around herself for protection against the cold.

She was always the first up, and it therefore it lay upon her to get the fire going, as well as the wood stove.

She didn't begrudge her father a little extra lay-in. He was a hard-worker and did a lot for the community.

She snatched up the lantern and it lighted her path toward the kitchen where she started the fire on the stove in preparation for her father's morning coffee.

Filling the kettle with water, Melody startled at a noise behind her. She put her hands to her chest and turned.

"Oooh, you startled me, Father," she said, almost breathless. "You're up early. I haven't even got to the main fire yet."

He waved her concerns aside. "I can do it," he said. "Something woke me, and I couldn't get back to sleep."

She stared at him. "You look a little pale, Father. Are you alright?"

He slapped at his cheeks. "Just a little tired. I feel fine." He went to light the fire in the front rocm.

Melody set out the cups and prepared to make her father's breakfast. Bacon and eggs today. They were blessed with twelve fine chickens, which not only supplied their own daily needs, but provided enough eggs to allow them to make a small stipend on the side.

By the time breakfast was served, the kettle had boiled and the coffee was ready.

"Fire's done," Jonas Harken announced as he re-entered the kitchen. "This looks wonderful, Melody," he said, breathing in the aromas of the freshly-cooked meal. "A good breakfast is a great start."

Melody rolled her eyes. As the only doctor in town, her father was forever spouting the benefits of a good breakfast to start the day. Sometimes it grated on her.

She often wondered if her mother had felt this way. Her dear mother had left this earth when Melody was only a teenager, leaving her to fill the void.

At twenty-seven, the expectation was she'd be married by now, but it wasn't to be. Her father told her he needed her here. Who else would look after the house and make the meals?

She was also needed in his busy medical practice. Although not formally trained, Melody acted as his nurse. Assisting where necessary, checking stocks, and billing patients.

She was an integral part of his business, and he had told her time and again he couldn't run his practice without her.

That wasn't quite true – he could employ a trained nurse, but then he'd have to pay her.

Doctor Harken checked his pocket-watch, the one his father had given him when he'd earned his medical certificate. "My first patient is due in ten minutes. Is the surgery ready?"

It was Melody's responsibility to ensure everything was in its place before each patient arrived. She led a very busy life looking after her father, and sometimes it got her down. "Yes, Father. I always prepare the room the evening before."

She looked at him quizzically. He knew that – she'd always worked that way. It took time to prepare the room, and she was generally too busy in the mornings to set it all up for the day.

"Good. Good," he muttered.

"Are you sure you're alright, Father? Your skin is almost white."

He waved her away, wiping the perspiration from his forehead. "Unlock the surgery door, and don't concern yourself about me," he said impatiently. "My first patient will be here any moment now."

She did as she was told, concern for her father at the back of her mind, and it wasn't long before the first patient arrived.

Just once, it would be nice to be able to sit down and have a leisurely cup of coffee. Or have some time to knit, or even do nothing.

The thought left her the moment it entered her head. Melody's father had been more than generous, allowing her to stay here with him.

She received free food and lodgings in return for helping him out. What more could she ask for?

"You've broken your arm," Doctor Harken said abruptly. "What possessed you to climb on the roof?"

Melody was shocked at his tone. It was unlike her father to chastise a patient like this.

Charles Jenkins stared at him. "The roof was leaking, Doc! I had to fix it."

"Then hire a younger man to do it. You're far too old to be undertaking such a lark." He turned to his daughter. "Get me a splint and some bandages, Melody. And I'll need your help."

"Hold this," he barked, indicating the splint, as he began the bandaging.

He was more than half way through when he quietly told her to finish the job. Not that she wasn't capable, but it was unlike her father to want her to do the bandaging. He preferred to do it because he was much better at it.

She finished the job and helped Mr Jenkins down, and was about to send him on his way when she noticed her father.

He was sitting behind his enormous desk, clutching his chest. He was even more pale than he had been earlier, if that were possible.

"Father?" she asked frantically. "Are you alright?"

Charles Jenkins leaned in. "I don't think he is."

"Father?" Melody said again, now near hysterical. "What can I do to help you?"

She ran around to the other side of the desk and held her father, who was now slumped over the desk.

Mr Jenkins came to stand next to her and leaned in. "I think it's too late," he said softly. "I believe he's gone."

Melody sat opposite Miss Bethany Wilde of the *Mail Order Bride Agency* in Westlake, Wyoming.

After her father's demise, she was on the brink of homelessness.

The new doctor had arrived with his wife, and since the house came with the surgery, she had to move out. She'd always known it was a possibility but hadn't thought of the consequences if her father suddenly passed as he had.

Even the furniture was part of the package.

She'd thought for sure she'd be married with a family of her own by then. But it wasn't too be.

Doctor Flint had been lovely and had offered her time to sort her life out. She wasn't sure a month would be long enough, especially since much of that time would be spent teaching his wife the processes.

He'd offered her a small fee for her time. At first she refused, not being used to being paid, but he'd insisted.

She finally realized she may need money, as she had none she could call her own. As it turned out, her father had little, putting most of it back into the business.

"I have a couple of eligible young men looking for wives," Miss Bethany said. "Miss Harken… Melody? Are you listening?"

It had been a difficult time. The funeral had gone as well as could be expected, and all their friends and family had attended. But she'd not seen any of them since. Not only was she an orphan now, she felt totally abandoned by everyone she knew. People she thought she could rely on.

"I'm sorry – I was thinking about my father." She wiped a stray tear from her cheek.

Miss Bethany came around to her side of the desk and hugged her. "My dear, I'm very sorry for your loss. But the sooner we find you a husband, the better. Yes?"

Melody nodded, then sniffed, putting her handkerchief to her nose. "Yes, you're right," she said, stiffening her back. "But…" she sniffed again. "How many men would be willing to take an old spinster like me?"

Miss Bethany stared at her. "You're not *that* old!"

"I most certainly am! I am twenty-seven years old. I've not so much as been to coffee and cake with a man."

Miss Bethany's eyes opened wide in astonishment, but she quickly refrained herself. "Then we shall fix that, eh?"

She smiled, but Melody didn't think it was a genuine reaction. Over the years she'd learned to read people. When someone smiled or laughed meaningfully, tiny wrinkles appeared around their eyes. Miss Bethany's eyes didn't change.

Despite that, she did think the older woman had genuine intentions.

"Do you have any idea where you'd like to go, my dear?" She said returning to her desk. She shuffled some letters around in her hands. "I have several letters here that might be of interest."

"I don't want to go anywhere; I want to stay here – with my father."

She could see the pity in the other woman's eyes. "Unfortunately that isn't an option, my dear. But I do have some letters here." She pulled one to the top. "This young man is from a fairly new town called Dayton Falls. It's in Montana."

She handed the letter across to Melody. Her eyes scanned the well-formed words.

I am a thirty-two year old man. I am terribly lonely and need a wife.

Dayton Falls has mostly single men. The only women are married.

I probably should tell you I own the Post Office here. Apart from companionship, I need help with household chores and meals.

Kindest regards,

Peter Williams

Melody read the letter again, then glanced up at Miss Bethany. "I'll take this one. He sounds nice."

The older woman frowned. "He didn't send a photo, so I have no idea what he looks like." She reached for two more letters. "Read these two before making your decision."

But Melody didn't want to read any more. Peter Williams sounded nice. He didn't want her to work in the business, and she only had to attend to the household chores and meals. That suited her fine.

"No, I want this one."

Miss Bethany sighed.

Melody stared at her. "Did I do something wrong?"

"No, this is not unusual. I've found that once a young lady has made up her mind, she doesn't want to see more." She smiled grimly. "It's your choice, my dear. I just like to offer variety."

Melody nodded. She was happy with her choice. "So what happens now?"

"You write to him and, he'll write back. See if you are compatible, and if so, you make your way to Dayton Falls."

Clutching the letter, she stood and thanked Miss Bethany, then made her way out of the office.

She would write to Peter Williams tonight, and get things moving.

Chapter Two

To: Post Master, Dayton Falls

Dear Mr Williams,

I am Melody Harken. I'm twenty-seven years old and have never been married. My father recently died, and since the new doctor has taken over, I have to leave. I've been left homeless and destitute and am in desperate need of a husband to support me.

I can do all the housework and I'm a very good cook. I would be happy to become your wife.

Kindest regards,

Melody Harken

Pete Williams read the letter over again. She sounded perfect.

When the letter had arrived this morning, his heart rate accelerated. He stared down at the envelope for the longest time before opening it. It was addressed with the most perfect cursive he'd ever seen. She was obviously well-educated.

The slightest fragrance lingered on the paper, and he wondered if it was the essence of his betrothed.

His hands shaking, he'd ripped the envelope open. Could this be his new wife?

Now that he'd read the letter, he was almost certain she was.

He'd written to the mail order bride agency on a whim. He'd seen an advertisement in a newspaper that had arrived from Wyoming.

Dayton Falls didn't have their own newspaper office yet, and he wasn't convinced they ever would. The town was far too small to make it worthwhile. Perhaps in the future?

He rubbed his hands together. He was so close to securing a wife, and it was exciting.

Out of nowhere, an unwanted memory popped into his head.

Dayton Falls was to be a fresh start for Pete and his wife. Little did they know when they started on their exciting adventure a little over two years earlier, that Priscilla was pregnant. Complications set in, and not only did she lose the baby, but she also lost her life. The only doctor on the wagon train was unable to stop the bleeding, and his darling Prissy had slipped away in front of his eyes.

He'd begun to write back to Miss Melody Harken, to tell her to come to Dayton Falls. He would even include a train ticket for her and some money to buy meals along the way. It was a long trip from Wyoming, and he wouldn't expect her to fund it herself.

Unexpectedly, his eyes began to leak. Pete wiped a hand across them and pushed the paper aside.

With renewed thoughts of his darling Prissy, he couldn't do it. He wouldn't betray her memory. He loved her too much for that.

"But you said I had another two weeks." Melody was distraught.

She'd taught the doctor's wife everything she needed to know, and now they were tossing her out like a piece of garbage.

Doctor Flint turned away. "I'm sorry," he said, with no sign of emotion or apology whatsoever in his voice. "Things have changed."

It wasn't true. Melody knew it and so did Doctor Flint. "You're nothing but a liar," Melody said, moments before her hands flew to her mouth. She had never been so disrespectful in her life.

Then again, she'd never had anyone blatantly lie to her face before.

He glared at her. "Get your belongings together and leave. I want you gone tonight."

"Tonight? Where am I going to go at this late notice?" Tears streamed down her face. If only her father hadn't died like that. He hadn't even left a will, which meant the small amount of money in his bank account was untouchable. "I barely have enough money for a train ride." She sobbed.

Mrs Flint walked in, and Melody glared at her. "I supposed you know about this? It was probably your plan all along?"

The woman looked genuinely surprised. And confused. "What is going on?"

Before her husband could answer with some cock and bull story, Melody told her. "He's kicking me out. I have to leave by tonight."

"Is that true, Robert? You're throwing her out on the street?"

He glared at his wife, willing her to take his side. "It was always going to happen."

"Only not right now!" she screeched at him. "The poor girl has lost her father. She's taught me everything she knows, and you repay her like this?"

She went to Melody and hugged her. The woman seemed genuine, which was more than she could say for her vile husband.

"We'll sort this out," she whispered, then led Melody to her room. "Pack your things and I'll do what I can," she said, then left Melody to her get her belongings together. She didn't have a lot of clothes, she'd never needed much, but managed to fill a small trunk.

When she'd removed her father's belongings from his room after the funeral, she'd found her mother's wedding gown. It was so beautiful, and Melody had always dreamed of wearing it for her own wedding. But it had never eventuated.

She carefully folded it and added it to the trunk.

She cleared out her drawers and grabbed up the sole photograph of the family of three from her dresser. She gathered up what little jewelry she had, which included two necklaces that had belonged to her mother, as well as Mother's rings. She held them close to her heart.

They'd never been valued, so she had no idea what they were worth, but the sentimental value was what meant the most to her.

Placing her hairbrushes in her carpetbag, she threw in her nightgown and robe, some undergarments, and her slippers.

She snatched up two dresses from the trunk as a last minute thought, as well as the wedding gown, in case her trunk got lost somewhere along the way. If that happened, she'd at least have a back up.

"I'm really sorry, dear," Mrs Flint told her when she returned to the room. "I have no idea what has come over Robert."

What could she say? Mrs Flint seemed genuine in her concern. "Don't tell Robert, but here are a few extra dollars to tide you over." She looked down at the notes that had been shoved into her hands. Five whole dollars. "Do you know where you're going?"

Melody hesitated to take the money, but realized she needed it to survive. She quickly put it in her reticule along with the other money the doctor had paid her for her services. "I'll be alright.

Don't you worry about me." Tears stung the back of her eyes, but she was determined not to show her distress.

"I'll organise a driver to take you to the station. Are you ready?"

Melody straightened her back and squared her shoulders. She wasn't ready, far from it, but she would not show fear to this woman. She especially wouldn't let the horrid Doctor Flint see how much his actions had affected her.

Dragging the trunk behind her, Melody arrived on the train platform, purchased her ticket, and registered her luggage. She breathed a sigh of relief once she was seated, but knew it would be a long journey.

Mrs Flint had been so kind to her, unlike her horrid husband. In addition to transportation to the train station, she'd made some sandwiches and packed a few pieces of fruit. At the least, it meant Melody wouldn't need to buy food for a day or so.

She settled into her carriage, placing her carpetbag in the rack. She kept her reticule close.

"All Aboard!" She heard the station master call out, then the driver blew the whistle, and they were soon on their way.

Melody had many regrets of late, not the least being she was unable to let her potential husband know she was arriving.

The carriage driver had stopped at Miss Bethany's but the place was closed up for the day, so they continued on to the station.

She worried that Mr Williams would be most unhappy with her turning up out of the blue. But what choice did she have?

It wasn't her fault Doctor Flint had turned her out onto the street without notice. In an ideal situation she would have waited for his return letter assuring her he was willing to go ahead with the marriage.

Instead she would arrive in Dayton Falls in a few days time, unaccompanied, without much in the way of money, and having no idea if he would even agree to marry her.

She swallowed back a sob. What if he rejected her?

Tears threatened at the back of her eyes, but Melody furiously blinked them back. She couldn't afford to think about such things.

It did her no good to go down that dark path.

The train suddenly jerked and she was thrown forward, as was her reticule. It landed on the floor under the empty seat opposite.

As she reached for her reticule, a well-dressed man in his thirties entered the carriage. She sighed. She'd hoped to have the carriage to herself the entire trip.

He reached down and picked up her reticule, passing it over to her. "Thank you," she said quietly.

"You are most welcome," he said with a smile and a little bow, then helped her to her feet.

Such a gentleman.

She wondered if Mr Peter Williams would be so polite. She hoped so.

"Are you traveling alone," he asked, as he took the seat opposite.

She swallowed hard and stared at him.

He frowned. "I apologize, Miss."

"Melody," she said shakily. "Melody Harken." She reached out her hand, and he shook it.

"I'm truly sorry," he said. "I didn't mean to scare you." She still wasn't sure about this stranger. "I'm happy to escort you for as far as I'm going. You can't trust all train travelers."

"I, I'm going as far as Dayton Falls," she said, still not certain about this man who was a complete stranger to her, and very unsure she should have divulged such information. "Do you do this often? Look out for strange women, I mean?"

He smiled. "I have a sister about your age. I'd like to think other men would look out for her if she ever found herself alone in a train carriage."

She breathed a sigh of relief. He was quite charming.

"I'm going to Great Falls, by the way, which is a little further down the line. I can definitely keep an eye on you."

Her heart did a little flutter, and she suddenly felt safer. "Thank you so much, Sir."

"Johnston. George Johnston." He smiled again, then leaned back into his seat, pulling his hat down over his eyes.

Melody stared out the window for the next two hours or so, taking in the scenery, until it became dark outside. She nibbled on one of the sandwiches, and said a silent prayer of thanks to Mrs Flint for her foresight. It didn't take long for her to be lulled into a deep sleep by the constant movement of the train.

She woke up with a start when they pulled into a station somewhere down the line. Her companion was sitting opposite, his hat still over his eyes.

He slowly stretched his legs, pushing his hat back on his head. "Good morning."

"Good morning," she said, a little more animated than Mr Johnston.

He stared out the window. "Ah, Little River. We'll be here for thirty minutes exactly."

She also stared outside. It looked like a friendly little town.

"Shall I escort you off the train and we'll find the privy and perhaps take a quick stroll?"

"Why not? So long as we don't miss the train leaving." Why not indeed? It sounded so lovely after being cramped in the small carriage for more hours than she cared to recall.

He reached for her hand, and escorted her off the train. "Hold tight to your reticule," he told her. "You don't know what sort of scoundrels you might come across."

She pulled it closer. "Oh? I thought you would be there to protect me, Mr Johnston."

He stared at her momentarily. "Of course, Miss Harken. It's just a precaution." He smiled and she felt more comfortable.

He pulled out his pocket-watch and checked the time. "Ten o'clock precisely. We must be back here by ten twenty-five and no later."

She nodded. He was just what she needed, and had obviously done this before.

Leaving the train, she spotted the privy and headed there. Then they took a nice stroll along the creek, not far from town. "It looks like a lovely place," she said, hoping Dayton Falls was just as appealing.

As they strolled alongside the creek, Mr Johnston talked about his sister, and his family. Her arm was linked through his the entire time, and she felt safe, protected.

At precisely ten twenty-five, they arrived back at the train. Their tickets were checked and they were allowed to re-board.

The next leg of their journey had begun.

Melody was tiring of sleeping upright on an uncomfortable torn and dirty seat. She was certain Mr Johnston must be too, but neither of them complained.

He'd been a wonderful companion for her during the long and boring trip, for which she was very grateful.

With her food getting low, Melody had to consider the possibility of purchasing food at the next stop. She told Mr Johnston as much.

"Do you have enough money?" he asked.

Her head shot up. He'd not asked such a question before. "I have only a little," she said. It was not a complete lie, she didn't have a lot of money, but she had enough to see her through. Mrs Flint had seen to that. "A few coins at most," she added to convince him she wasn't flash with money.

He nodded but said nothing, then pulled his hat down over his eyes and went off to sleep.

Melody forced herself to stay awake a while longer. The more tired she was, the better quality of sleep she would have in this horrible contraption.

She pulled her reticule close to her chest and finally drifted off to sleep.

She awoke with a start some hours later to find the train pulling out of yet another station – Little Rock. Her companion was nowhere to be seen, and her reticule lay open on the seat next to her.

Melody scrambled to check her pocketbook and found it empty. Tears sprang to her eyes. He'd seemed so trustworthy, and yet...

She stared out of the window onto the platform. And there he stood, grinning at her and waving as the train continued its journey. She blinked and he was gone.

"You scoundrel," she shouted, using his exact words. It made her feel a little better, but did nothing to retrieve her lost money.

It was then she realized it was his plan all along — to gain her trust and then rob her. He seemed like such a nice man, caring and protective.

She fought back a sob. What a fool she'd been.

It seemed she was always being fooled lately. And all because her father had been selfish and hadn't thought about her future.

Scrounging through her carpetbag she found a lone apple. That would have to carry her over until they reached Dayton Falls the next morning.

At least he hadn't taken her most prized possession – her mother's wedding dress.

Chapter Three

His decision made, Postmaster Pete Williams put pen to paper. He could not marry Miss Melody Harken. Tarnishing his dead wife's memory was not an option.

He apologized for his change of mind, and wished her well. Pete decided against explaining his reasons, believing it may muddy the waters.

He reached for an envelope and addressed it. He was about to add the stamp when a telegram arrived.

He sighed. Right now he just wanted to get this over and done with and not have to worry again.

Copying the telegram down word for word, he then began to lock up. Hurrying to his destination, he heard the whistle blowing as the train pulled into the station.

He needed to hurry. He wanted to catch Edward Horvard from the Mercantile before he left his store unnecessarily.

"Ah Edward," he said, arriving just in time to see the man in question about to lock up his store. "A telegram. Unfortunately your supplies aren't arriving today."

He handed over the hastily written message.

Edward stared at it. "What a nuisance, but I guess it can't be helped. Thank you, Pete, appreciated." He nodded and returned to his store, taking down the sign that indicated he'd be back in half an hour.

Pete strolled back toward the post office, waving and smiling at the town folks along the way. Mrs Grogan, the doctor's wife, spotted him and crossed the road to chat. There was no way around it, he would just have to endure it.

It was always the same. "How are you coping without your dear Priscilla?" He knew she meant well, but after all this time, he wished she would stop.

She waved and walked hastily across the dirt road. "Mr Williams," she shouted, waving as she did so. "How are you coping without your dear Priscilla?"

If he could roll his eyes without her seeing he would. Instead he was forced to put a smile on his face. "Good morning, Mrs Grogan. How are you today?" He'd learned to ignore her question and completely change the subject.

"I'm perfectly fine, thank you, Mr Williams." She looked him up and down. "I believe you've lost more weight. Are you eating properly?"

He inwardly groaned. Was she serious? How did she expect him to eat properly when he didn't know how to cook much more than bacon and eggs and beans.

"I guess so." What else could he say to a direct question like that? He really didn't want to lie to the woman.

"Mr Simpson has lamb shanks on special today. You could make yourself a nice little supper with a couple of those."

It was enough to make his mouth water. "Thank you, Mrs Grogan. I'll keep it in mind." He had no intention of doing any such thing, but it would keep her off his back. "I really must go. It looks like I have a customer waiting outside the door."

He could see her in the distance, but didn't recognize her as a local. A visitor to town perhaps? Probably got off the train.

"Of course, of course. Good day to you, Mr Williams."

With that she was on her way again. Pete breathed a sigh of relief and headed toward the Post Office and his mysterious customer.

Melody pulled the crinkled letter out of her pocket. She'd need some proof she was who she said she was.

She turned the door handle but the door wouldn't budge. She'd been through so much not only on her way here, but in the weeks since her father had died leaving her destitute.

Her embarrassment at her situation was overwhelming.

She heard the man before she saw him. "I won't be a moment," he said, almost running to let her in. "I had to deliver a telegram."

He was out of breath, but smiled, and she was immediately drawn to him. He seemed a friendly sort of chap. Good looking too. Was this the man she was to marry?

"Good morning, Ma'am." He unlocked the door and allowed her entrance.

She smiled back. Her relief at finally arriving in Dayton Falls was palpable. "Thank you, it's Miss. I'm looking for Mr Peter Williams."

He stopped dead in his tracks and his face went white as a sheet. "That is I," he said, his voice shaking. "And who might be asking?"

His expression told her he already knew who she was. She reached out her hand. "Miss Melody Harken. I wrote to you."

He went even whiter, if that was possible. "You can't be," he said quietly. "I haven't written back yet." He stood stark still, not moving even a fraction. "That is, I have written, today, but I haven't posted the letter yet."

He reached across the counter and snatched up an envelope. Melody stared at it. Her name and address were neatly written on the envelope.

"I was about to put a stamp on it when an urgent telegram arrived," he explained. But that didn't really explain anything.

Was he trying to tell her something?

She reached over and snatched the letter out of his hands. The horror on his face said it all. Without warning, he grabbed it back.

"Is there a reason you don't want me to read your letter," she asked, straightening her back, fearing the worst.

She caught him off guard and stole the letter back again, this time rushing out the door, and tearing it open.

He followed her.

Melody came to a sudden halt when she read the words explaining he couldn't marry her after all. She slowly turned around to face him, fighting back the tears that threatened to spill over her face.

"I've come such a long way," she said, barely above a whisper. "I spent days on that horrid train, and was robbed of all my money. The little I had."

She headed toward the post office to collect the trunk she'd left outside the building. He followed her. "I have nothing," she whispered, and this time the tears fell like waterfalls. There was no holding them back, no matter how much she tried.

"The new doctor threw me out on the street without warning, and I had to leave that same day." She straightened her back again, and wiped at the tears flooding her cheeks. "Is there a boarding house here? Not that I have any money to pay for it."

She watched as his face softened.

"No boarding house, only a hotel." He took a few steps toward her until they were only inches apart. He looked genuinely worried for her. "I'm happy to pay for a room for you, and your ticket back home, of course."

He reached out and wiped her cheeks. His touch was gentle, and he did seem to care. Or did he?

She swallowed hard. "There is no home. I have nowhere to go."

"Nowhere? What are you…"

"I am homeless," she said, interrupting him. "My father died with no will, and I have nothing but what I've arrived here with."

His eyes opened wide. "Nothing?" He seemed shocked. "He left you with nothing? What a cad."

She felt the heat rise from her neck to her face. "My father died suddenly. He didn't expect to die for many years." She was near-screaming, and felt her hysteria rising. Tears began to flow again, much to her disgust. The fact her belly was empty didn't help.

She watched as he glanced around. He had no idea what to do with a hysterical woman, that much was clear.

He seemed like a decent man, but he'd obviously decided not to marry her, going by the letter, and now she was stuck in a town she didn't know, with people who didn't care.

Her bottom lip quivered and she felt faint. The combination of the shock of being jilted and the emptiness of her belly were surely contributing factors.

"I, I need to sit down, Mr Williams," she said quietly. "I feel rather faint."

The look of horror crossed his face once more. His arm suddenly went up, and he waved to someone across the way. "Mrs Grogan," he called. "Do you have a moment?"

His arm went around her waist, supporting her, and she felt somewhat comforted. The last thing she needed was to collapse in a strange place with a man she barely knew. Even if that man was meant to be her husband.

Her last memory was of two strong arms reaching underneath her and picking her up.

Melody's eyes blinked open.

"How long since you ate, Miss Harken?"

It was a woman's voice. An unfamiliar voice.

Melody looked around. She had no idea where she was. "Eaten? I had an apple yesterday."

"My dear girl, that is not enough! It's no wonder you fainted."

She felt compelled to explain. "I, I was robbed on the train. That was to be my food money for the last leg of the trip."

The woman gasped. "Oh my goodness, you poor thing." She brushed Melody's hair back off her face. "I'm Mrs Grogan, the doctor's wife," she said hastily. "Mr Williams, the young lady needs food."

Mrs Grogan stood.

"But I have no money…"

"Don't you worry about money. Mr Williams will pay." She turned toward Melody's betrothed.

He shuffled forward. "Yes, of course I will," he said, looking far more like he'd rather not.

"Sit up slowly, and we'll see how you go. If you faint again, I'll get my husband over here."

That was more than enough incentive for her to take it slowly and not risk fainting again. She really didn't want another stranger involved.

She sat on the side of the bed for nearly a minute, then Mrs Grogan helped her up. Mr Williams rushed in, shoving some notes into Mrs Grogan's hands.

The older woman led her down the road to what turned out to be known as *Edna's Diner*. The place was near empty, and they had their choice of tables.

Mrs Grogan led her to a cubicle at the back, away from prying eyes, no doubt, and Edna soon joined them.

"Good morning, Mrs Grogan. What will it be?" She looked curiously at Melody. Vying for an introduction no doubt.

"Two white teas, bacon and eggs for Miss Harken. Oh, and toast. She needs a decent feed."

Edna nodded and walked back to the kitchen.

While they waited, Mrs Grogan pried every detail of her life since her father had died. It wasn't pretty. "You poor girl," she said, patting Melody's hand. "You've been through so much."

Melody said nothing. She was certain tears would begin to flow again if she said another word.

"And that Mr Johnston. What a scoundrel! We shall tell our dear Sheriff Doyle. He'll put out an alert."

Her breakfast arrived, and Melody leaned into the aroma. Her mouth was watering from the smell alone.

"Go on, eat up," Mrs Grogan told her, taking a sip of tea. "It looks very appetizing."

She glanced down into the huge plate of food. Melody had never had seen such a large breakfast, let alone eaten one that big. She tucked in eagerly. She hadn't eaten in over twenty-four hours. No wonder she fainted!

"This is lovely," she said, taking another bite.

Mrs Grogan smiled. "I'm sure it will help." She took another sip of her tea. "It's lovely having a fresh new face in Dayton Falls. You'll make a lovely wife for our Mr Williams."

Melody stopped with her fork mid-way to her mouth. "He doesn't want to marry me."

"He will." The doctor's wife had such a smug look on her face, Melody was almost convinced.

She didn't want to marry a man who didn't want her, but how would she survive? At twenty-seven, her options were severely limited.

"I feel so much better, Mrs Grogan. Thank you." Melody wiped her mouth with the linen napkin in her lap.

"Don't thank me, my dear. Mr Williams paid for it. And so he should – such a scoundrel, leading you on like that!"

She could see the older woman was becoming agitated and changed the subject. "I'll arrange for my trunk to be moved to the hotel, and get settled in there." She began to stand. "Mr Williams has offered to pay. After that, I have no idea what I'll do."

The older woman stood with her. "I have a better idea. Why don't you come and stay with Dr Grogan and me. We have a spare room, and could do with some help around the place."

"Oh, I couldn't…"

After she'd paid for the meal, Mrs Grogan turned to face her. "You could, and I'd like you too. Frankly I'm getting too old for this caper. Helping my husband in the clinic all day, then making the meals at night. Not to mention cleaning the house." She sighed. "I'm tired. I've had enough."

Melody stared at her. She seemed genuine enough.

"As long as you're sure?"

Mrs Grogan put her arm around Melody. "I'm absolutely certain. My husband will be happy too. He'll finally get someone who knows what they're doing to help out in the clinic."

Melody nodded.

"We'll pay you a small stipend, of course."

Melody stopped walking. "Board and lodgings is more than enough."

"We'll see." She smiled at Melody and they continued on their way to the post office.

"Mr Williams," Mrs Grogan said assertively. "Miss Harken will be staying with Dr Grogan and myself. Please make arrangements for her trunk to be delivered."

He reached behind the counter and handed Melody her carpetbag. "You're not staying at the hotel? I said I would pay."

"And so you should," Mrs Grogan said, thoroughly irritated. "Leading the poor girl on like that. You ought to be ashamed of yourself."

Mr Williams bent his head. Perhaps he did feel a little guilty. "I'm very sorry, Miss Harken. It was never my intention to…"

"Good day, Mr Williams!" Mrs Grogan turned tail and headed out the door.

When they got outside she turned to Melody. "Serve him right, leading you on like that."

"I'm sure he didn't mean it. I arrived unexpectedly, after all."

Mrs Grogan waved her hand across her body. "Let's not worry about him now. Lord knows he needs a wife after… Oh dear. Forget I said anything."

Melody frowned. Was there something she should know?

"Here we are." She let herself into the large log cabin sitting on the outskirts of the main street. *Medical Centre* burned into a wooden sign, which hung over the main door.

"Henry, this is Miss Melody Harken. She'll be staying with us for a while." She gave him no choice, and Dr Grogan nodded.

"Hello," he said, frowning.

"She's a doctor's daughter, and we need help." Mrs Grogan then showed Melody to her room, giving the doctor no chance to object.

It was clean and tidy. A little smaller than the room she'd had back in Westlake, but big enough. It contained a wardrobe, an armchair, and a single bed that was made up ready for guests. There was also a small table next to the bed containing a lantern.

"There's a spare blanket in the wardrobe should you need it. Towels are in the bathroom cupboard." Melody sat on the side of the bed. It was comfortable. After the harrowing time she'd spent on the train, she knew she'd sleep well tonight.

She might not be a bride, but a comfortable and safe night's sleep was just as important to her at the moment.

"Settle yourself in, and I'll be back in a while to show you around."

Melody felt more wanted now than she had in several weeks, but wondered what the future held for her. Mr Peter Williams certainly didn't want her, just like Doctor Robert Flint.

She had no idea what her life would be two days from now, let alone two weeks.

Chapter Four

Pete closed up the Post Office for lunch. He would deliver Miss Harken's trunk to the medical center, then wipe his hands of the whole sorry saga.

Why on earth he'd sent that letter, he'd never know. The last thing he needed was a bride. And a mail order bride, a complete stranger? What was he thinking?

He mentally slapped himself. He knew exactly what he was thinking. He was lonely. He was also sick of eating beans and bacon, and the occasional eggs.

Mrs Grogan was right when she'd said he'd lost more weight. He'd had to tighten his belt yet again, and it wasn't something that made him happy.

He'd never been overweight, but this was a first, being so far underweight. People didn't understand that what he did was physical. Adding mail to pigeon-holes all day. Reaching up and down, moving boxes, running around to deliver telegrams – it was hard work.

Despite that, he enjoyed what he did.

But he'd craved companionship. Did that mean he needed a wife? Perhaps.

Or maybe not.

It was more than two years since he'd lost his precious Priscilla, and if he was truthful with himself, it was his fault. If not for him, she wouldn't have been pregnant, wouldn't have lost the baby, and subsequently bled to death.

He wiped a trembling hand across his eyes.

The guilt was what made him change his mind. How could he even contemplate a new bride, when he lay awake each and every night thinking about his beautiful Priscilla?

He locked the Post Office door and snatched up the trunk, trying to force his mind onto other things.

Without warning, Miss Harken entered his thoughts. He wondered what she was doing now.

Was she sitting and laughing with Mrs Grogan, drinking tea, or perhaps wandering around town?

As much as the older woman grated on him at times, she was there when he needed her. He was well aware she'd do anything for anyone who needed help.

He understood that from first-hand experience. She'd helped him through after Priscilla's death, and was there again today.

Melody's face flashed into his mind. She was such a pretty girl. She had a softness about her looks, despite everything she'd been through.

He'd like to get his hands on that scoundrel who robbed her!

Whoa! She was not his problem.

He forced his mind away from Miss Harken, and carried the trunk to its destination. He knocked on the door and waited for Mrs Grogan to answer.

He put the trunk down while he waited.

He could hear voices coming from inside, so knew someone was there. The aroma of freshly baked bread drifted through the door.

His mouth watered.

The door suddenly opened. Melody Harken stared momentarily at him. "Thank you for bringing the trunk, Mr Williams."

She stood there in the open doorway, with the face of an angel. Miss Melody Harken, according to her letter, was a twenty-seven year old spinster.

But there was nothing spinsterish about her. Her wavy brown hair, her blue eyes that reminded him of bluebells, her luscious pink lips.

He mentally slapped himself. He needed to snap out of it. "I, I have your trunk," he said, stuttering like a love-struck schoolboy.

"Through here, Mr Williams." She led him to a room at the back of the house. She hovered just outside the room as he placed the trunk inside. It wouldn't be right for them both to be in her bedroom at the same time.

"Thank you." She immediately led him back through the house and past the kitchen. The delicious aromas hit his senses again.

He was about to leave when Mrs Grogan came running out, breathless. "Mr Williams," she called to him. "There is beef and vegetable soup on the stove, and freshly baked bread - just out of the oven. Stay for luncheon?"

He hesitated.

"As a thank you for bringing the trunk."

What did he have to lose? He had to eat anyway. "That would be lovely. Thank you Mrs Grogan."

She grinned. "Don't thank me – Miss Harken did all the work."

He very nearly backed off, but his belly rumbled at the pleasant aromas coming from the kitchen.

"Sit yourself down, Mr Williams." He did as he was told. After all this time in Dayton Falls, this was the first time he'd been in the Grogan's kitchen.

Mrs Grogan had delivered food to him many a time, but he'd never eaten here.

Doc Grogan arrived moments later, and after giving thanks for their food, they began to eat. "This is amazing, Miss Harken. You're an excellent cook."

"I've been cooking for my father for many years," she said softly, and a sadness came across her face. "More bread?"

He wouldn't say no. It was delicious, probably the best he'd ever eaten. He emptied his soup bowl, and wiped it out with a piece of bread.

Before he could object, the bowl was whipped away, refilled, and placed in front of him again.

"You're spoiling me." But he wouldn't say no. It was probably the best meal he'd had for a very long time.

The two women turned to each other and grinned.

"You don't cook for yourself, Mr Williams. You're far too skinny – Miss Harken's soup will help get you through the day."

It was fact. His weight loss was worrying, but not unexpected. "I do appreciate it, and it is quite delicious." He tucked in again.

He could certainly get used to this. Too bad he'd changed his mind about marrying Miss Melody Harken – she was a really good cook.

Dear Mr Williams,

Would you be kind enough to accompany Miss Harken to church on Sunday? Oh, and we are expecting you at luncheon again tomorrow. See you at noon?

Regards,

Mrs Bertha Grogan

The letter had been slipped under the post office door sometime after closing.

Pete read the letter over again. He hadn't misread it – was he being set up? Surely the old lady wouldn't do that? She knew how much Priscilla had meant to him.

Luncheon did sound wonderful though, especially if it was as good as yesterday. He hadn't minded having beans and bacon for supper last night. After such a special meal in the middle of the day, he hadn't even been all that hungry.

And he'd slept better last night than he had since... He shook the thoughts away.

He checked his pocket-watch. It was almost time for him to lock up for luncheon. He spun around as the door opened.

"Miss Harken. I didn't expect to see you here."

She laughed and the sound made his heart sing. "I should be in the kitchen, do you mean?"

That really was what he meant, and perhaps he was a little disappointed she was here now and not tending to the food. "Did Mrs Grogan cook today?"

"No, that was me. Everything is under control, and Mrs Grogan asked if I could bring these letters for posting."

He stared at her momentarily. "I could have brought them back with me."

She slapped her hands to her mouth in surprise. "Silly me. What was I thinking?"

What was she thinking indeed? She handed the pile of letters over, as well as the money for stamps. "I'll only be a few minutes if you'd like to wait? We can walk together."

She smiled and her whole face lit up. "I'd like that."

He saw to the letters, then took his coat from the rack, then pulled it around himself. "Do you have a coat, Miss Harken?" he asked concerned.

"I do have one back at the Grogan's."

"The closer we get to Christmas, the colder it gets," he said, as they stepped out the door and he locked up.

"Oh, it is quite chilly. I'll have to fetch my coat next time."

He pulled off his coat and offered it to her. "Oh, I couldn't," she said, brushing it aside.

"I insist, Miss Harken." He draped his warm woolen coat over her shoulders, and they began their short journey.

"Tell me about yourself, Miss Harken," he said amiably. "What did you do for your father? And what happened on that train?"

She hooked her arm through his, and told him about the horrid Mr Johnston, and he was appalled. That a so-called gentleman could do such a thing to a lady, was beyond reprehensible.

He felt comfortable in the company of the captivating Miss Harken, but knew he shouldn't.

"And here we are, Mr Williams." She turned to him and he found himself staring into those stunning bluebell-colored eyes.

It was difficult to pull his gaze away, and he swallowed hard. What was he doing? He had no interest whatsoever in this woman.

This beautiful woman with silky brown hair, with waves the like of which he'd never seen before. Despite all her recent sad history and let downs, she was still very likeable, and sociable. If he hadn't decided not to marry again, things could be different.

She leaned forward and opened the front door, leading him into the kitchen. Doc Grogan sat at the heavy wooden table awaiting his meal.

"Nice to see you again, Mr Williams."

Melody took the coat from her shoulders and placed it on the coat rack. "Sit yourself down, Mr Williams," she told him. "Luncheon won't be long."

She flicked her long hair back over her shoulders, then turned toward the stove. As she opened the oven door, the enticing aroma hit his senses.

"That smells divine," he said before he could stop himself.

Miss Harken smiled. "Lamb shank stew," she said. "I hope you like it." She dished the food out onto two plates for the men, then set a plate in front of him.

He leaned into it and breathed it in.

Once the women sat down with their food, they all linked hands and said thanks for the food and the opportunity to spend time together.

"I could get used to this," he told the others. The two women turned to each other and smiled. Just like they'd done the day before.

He took a mouthful of food and savored it. "Miss Harken, Mrs Grogan, you are amazing cooks." He ate another mouthful, and then another. He thanked the Lord for bringing Miss Harken to Dayton

Falls. And for the opportunity of companionship with these compassionate people.

In the back of his mind he heard a little voice that reminded him *he'd* brought her to Dayton Falls. It also told him he didn't want her.

If he'd been alone he would surely have argued with that little voice. He'd have told it that was before he knew her.

"Oh!" Miss Harken suddenly jumped up from the table and placed a tray of freshly baked bread on the table. "Would you mind cutting the bread, Mr Williams?" she asked, pushing the tray toward him, along with a sharp knife.

How could he say no? He did as asked, and felt her eyes on him the whole time. It was all he could do not to reciprocate.

"There you are – all done," he said as he sat back down at the table.

"You get first slice since you did such a wonderful job." She laughed that enticing tinkling sound that drew him in so much, and his heart fluttered.

He reached for a plate and a slice of bread, not taking his eyes off her for a moment. "Thank you, Miss Harken."

"You may call me Melody," she said softly.

"Oh, I couldn't," he said. "It wouldn't be right." She pouted and he immediately regretted his words. "Perhaps I could after all, if that's really what you want," he added reluctantly. "Then you should call me Pete."

She smiled , then went back to her food.

"About Sunday," he said after he'd finished his lamb shank stew. "Are you not going to church, Mrs Grogan?"

"We always..." Doc Grogan began to say, but his wife interrupted him.

"I'm not certain we'll be there, so if you could escort Miss Harken, er, Melody, that would be wonderful."

And so it was settled. He would pick her up and get her safely to church on Sunday morning. If he didn't know better, he'd think there was some sort of scheming going on. One that pushed him toward Melody. But since she was now working for Doc Grogan, he must be imagining it.

Chapter Five

Sunday soon came around.

He'd enjoyed luncheon with the Grogan's and Melody every day, and was quickly getting used to it. The strangest part was how they'd suddenly taken to inviting him there each day, when they'd never done so before.

Not that Pete was complaining. He was feeling healthier, and sleeping much better with real food in his belly instead of sandwiches and beans most days. Last night he'd cooked bacon, eggs and toast. The toast was a little burned, but he didn't care.

The rest of the food was fine.

Mrs Grogan had sent him home yesterday with a slice of pound cake to have with his supper. It was very nice. No doubt Melody had made that too.

He sat at the breakfast table and finished his coffee. The empty bowl from his oatmeal sat on the table waiting to be washed.

Life had changed considerably since Melody had arrived, and he wondered how long it would last. Mrs Grogan had said she wanted to retire. She'd had enough of looking after Doc Grogan's business, and so Melody was taking over.

That made sense, but what about the doc? Was he giving up too? If that were the case, the town would have to start looking for another doctor to take over. It wasn't easy to get doctors out to these remote areas.

His head hurt. He was thinking too much, about things that might not ever happen.

He cleaned up from breakfast, put on his tie and jacket, then reached for his warm woolen coat, his thick gloves, and his hat. He hoped Melody wore her warm coat today. In fact, he would insist on it. With only a few weeks until Christmas, snow would begin to fall soon, and the temperature would be icy cold.

As he reached the medical center, he knocked on the door. It wasn't long before Melody opened it wide.

He looked her up and down. The emerald green skirt matched with an embroidered white shirt looked so refreshing on her. She had her thick coat over her arm.

"You'll need to put that on before we leave," he told her sternly. "It's freezing outside."

She ducked her head through the door. "No snow though." She looked disappointed.

"No, but it's not far off. I suspect we could have snow before the end of the week, if not the end of the day."

She grinned. "I've never seen snow," she said, her eyes wide. "It will be fun."

"Not really," he muttered. He took her coat and helped her into it. She pulled her gloves onto her peaches and cream hands, and pulled her hat down over her head.

As he stepped away from the door, she linked her arm through his, and they began their stroll toward the church.

"It's not very far, but it's hidden behind the town."

She glanced at him. "I'm excited to see the Dayton Falls church. I've heard it's lovely. And very friendly too."

Without thinking, he patted her hand. "Yes, very welcoming. Everyone in this small town is friendly and sociable. That's what I love about it."

"But you don't socialize much." It was a statement, not a question. Obviously Mrs Grogan had been gossiping about him.

"Did Mrs Grogan tell you that?" Melody didn't answer so he continued. "I suppose she told you everything else as well?

She frowned. At least that much was sacred.

"She didn't tell me much, just that you don't get out much, and don't look after yourself."

"I guess that's something." They rounded the corner and could see the church in the distance. As they got closer, they could hear the sounds of *How Great Thou Art* coming from inside.

Melody sighed. "One of my most favorite hymns," she said. "My mother loved it too."

He reached over and squeezed her hand. She stared down at their entwined hands, and he suddenly snatched it away. He'd overstepped the mark.

They took their place in the back row of the pews, and he saw unshed tears in Melody's eyes. She obviously missed her mother a lot.

She pulled off her gloves and took up one of the bibles sitting on the ledge for use by parishioners. She quickly turned the pages and sat reading silently when she found what she wanted.

Melody was deep in thought and only closed the bible when the music stopped.

"Move across please, Mr Williams." It was Doc and Mrs Grogan. So much for not coming along today. He slid across, along with Melody.

Today's sermon was about friendship and community. That was one of the things he loved about this lovely little town – you were never truly alone. There was always someone there in your hour of need.

Take Mrs Grogan for example. She had apparently recognized a need in him, and had acted on it. He turned to face her, and she glanced across at him, nodding her recognition at her part in what the preacher was saying.

He would have to make a point to say an extra thank you after the service.

At the end of the service, they all filed out the door, thanking the preacher as they did so. "Preacher Brown," Pete said. "I'd like to introduce Miss Melody Harken."

"What brings you here, Miss Harken?" the preacher asked, and Pete held his breath. Would she say it was to marry him?

She glanced sideways at him. "I'm helping Doctor and Mrs Grogan," she said confidently, and Pete breathed a huge sigh of relief.

Everyone mingled after church, and some stayed for tea or coffee. Over the past few weeks, there'd been talk of having luncheon after church, where everyone brought a plate of food.

Melody thought that was a wonderful idea, and so did Mrs Grogan. Most of the congregation was made up of men, and they didn't agree.

The small handful of women in town had come on the wagon train when the town was founded. It was mostly made up of single men, and a few married couples with young children.

The thought had Pete swallowing hard. If Priscilla had survived, they'd have a toddler running around now, and perhaps even another baby on the way. He'd be a father now, and wouldn't be fighting with himself because of overwhelming guilt.

When it was time to leave, Mrs Grogan accosted him. "I'm so sorry about this morning," she said. "I've been feeling a little unwell these past days, and wasn't sure I'd make it this morning."

Pete stared at her. "Nothing serious I hope?"

She waved a hand across in front of her. "I'm fine now." She glanced across at one of the other wives. "Would you mind walking Melody home? I'd like to catch up with Mrs Green. I'm not sure how long I will be."

"Oh, Mrs Green," she said, waving and walking away. "Thank you Mr Williams," she said over her shoulder, not waiting for an answer.

He joined the younger woman who was chatting to some of the Ladies Auxiliary members. "Miss Harken has agreed to join us," Mrs Jensen said, grinning. "I've heard she's a wonderful cook, and will be such a wonderful asset to the auxiliary."

Melody hooked her arm through his, which was not lost on Mrs Jensen. "She is indeed," he said. "I can attest to that."

"Oh?" Mrs Jensen's eyes opened wide.

"We, ah, we have to go," he said quickly, not wanting to answer her unasked question. The older women in town were always trying to marry him off.

Not that there were any suitable women about. Melody happened to be the only single woman in town right now. And that wasn't an option. He'd already rejected her.

She turned and stared into his face. Her hair fell across her eyes, and it was all he could do to stop himself from brushing it back behind her ear.

What was wrong with him? He'd made his decision – he wasn't getting married again. And that was the end of that.

They chatted about anything and everything as he walked Melody home. She told him about her father's sudden death, and what it had done to her.

She was still finding her way around town, so he pointed out the various stores, and told her who owned them. She peered through the window of the Mercantile, but vowed to go in there sometime and take a look around.

Not that she could buy anything, she'd told him. After her father's demise she had very little, but the man who robbed her on the train took the small amount she'd had.

He felt anger boil up inside him. What a low act to do that to someone already in a desperate situation.

She should be grateful, she told him. Mr Johnston, if that was even his real name, had left her carpetbag in tact.

It contained her mother's wedding dress, which she'd planned to wear for their wedding ceremony.

Guilt hit him square in the heart.

That poor girl had come here with the expectation that he would marry and support her. Instead he rejected her. This was all his fault.

He swallowed back the emotion that threatened to change his mind.

He was about to apologize when they arrived at the medical center. She unlocked the door and he turned to walk away when he saw Doctor and Mrs Grogan in the distance.

"Mr Williams. Mr Williams!" Mrs Grogan waved to him at the same time she shouted. "Don't go, Mr Williams," she called as she got closer.

She rushed forward and was out of breath by the time she arrived. "Stay for luncheon? We're having roast lamb. It's already in the oven."

He opened his mouth to speak, but Mrs Grogan beat him to it. "There is far too much for the three of us. I implore you to stay, Mr Williams."

As the front door opened, the aroma of a roast cooking in the oven hit him. How could he say no to that?

"It does smell wonderful," he said softly. "But I feel I have imposed enough on your hospitality of late."

He turned and began to walk away.

"Please?" It was a gentle plea, but one he felt he couldn't ignore.

He turned to face the amazingly beautiful Melody. Her hair had fallen across her face again, and he lifted his hand to chase it back.

Her eyes were mesmerizing him. He had no right to touch this woman, and he dragged his hand away.

They all stood on the pathway from the gate to the house, and Mrs Grogan was nodding her head and grinning.

What was there to be grinning about?

He hesitated.

"Do stay, Mr Williams," the older woman said firmly. "We do so enjoy your company. Besides, what else will you have for luncheon? Some left over beans?"

She was frowning, and he knew she was right.

"I do enjoy the food, and the company," he said equally as firmly. "But I fear I have imposed for far too long."

Melody stepped inside the house. "I was hoping we could go for another stroll this afternoon. After we'd eaten."

His restraint was being sorely tested. "This afternoon?"

She nodded. "It's not too cold with our coats on. And if it does snow, I don't want to miss it."

Mrs Grogan frowned. She had no inkling of their earlier discussion.

"Perhaps we could venture further out. I'd like to collect some pine branches and pine cones to make some Christmas decorations."

Mrs Grogan clapped her hands. "That would be wonderful, my dear." The look on her face told him the idea was a hit.

How could he deny her that joy? "If everyone is in agreeance, then I accept your generous offer. Thank you."

They all moved into the house, and the two men went into the sitting room while the women prepared the gravy and dished up the luncheon.

"So, Doc," Pete said staring across at the doctor. "Are you retiring too?"

"Retiring? Me? I have no plans for it. What's brought this on?"

Pete was confused. "With Mrs Grogan retiring, I naturally thought..."

"Ah," the older man said, as though it suddenly all made sense. "Mrs Grogan isn't retiring. She's just utilizing Melody's expertise until..." He suddenly stopped talking, then floundered. "I, I'm sure it will be short-lived."

Pete frowned and was about to ask further questions when they were called into the kitchen to eat.

"It smells amazing. You ladies have done a wonderful job."

Mrs Grogan stared at him. "I'm not a very good cook," she said. "This is all Melody."

"She's an excellent cook," the doctor added. "I don't know what we'll do when she's gone."

His wife glared at him.

"That is, when she eventually goes. Hopefully not for a long time."

A plate was placed in front of the men, and then the women sat down with their meals. They all linked hands and said prayers of thanks for the food and companionship.

After today's sermon, Pete felt the companionship meant much more to him than it had yesterday. And for that he was grateful.

"Mmmm, this is delicious. I wish I had someone cooking like this for me."

Mrs Grogan grinned. "But you do, Mr Williams. And you could have had her all to yourself."

She was right. He could have had Melody as his wife, but he refused. He rejected her despite inviting her to marry him.

What kind of fool was he?

"I'm very sorry, Miss Harken," he said, reverting back to formality. "I did the wrong thing, and I apologize."

"Apology accepted," she said, then went back to her food as though it meant nothing to her.

Chapter Six

She graciously accepted his apology, when what Melody really wanted to do was scream at him.

But young ladies do not act that way. Besides, Mrs Grogan explained that gently gently was the way to go.

She had to show Mr Peter Williams that she was flexible, and was willing to forgive him for his indiscretions when they first met.

And besides that, he seemed to be warming to her. Wasn't that what she wanted?

She'd sat opposite him at the table, and stole glances his way when possible.

From the moment she'd set eyes on him, she'd known he was a kind man, even if he was indecisive. He was also very handsome, with his dirty blond hair, as she liked to call it. Not quite brown, but darker than blond, it sat just below his collar. A little long, but not too long.

His blue eyes pierced her whenever he glanced her way. It was as though he was trying to see down into her soul.

"That was lovely, Miss Harken," he said as he wiped his mouth with the linen napkin. He stood, taking his plate with him.

"Oh no, Mr Williams," she said quickly. "That is my job. Please sit down and let me clear the table."

After all, as his wife, that's what she would do. She'd done that exact same thing for her father from the time her mother had died, so it wasn't as though she wasn't used to it.

Heat crept up his face, then he nodded and took his seat again.

They were dancing around each other – one not wanting to upset the other – and it felt a little precarious, to say the least.

She finished her last mouthful of food, then scooted around to the other side of the table, and cleared the dishes away.

"My belly is full," he said as he smiled at her. "You are an excellent cook."

She was disappointed and frowned. "I've made dessert," she said sadly. "I hope you're not too full for that?"

"I, er,"

"Take the pie out of the oven, Miss Harken," Mrs Grogan directed. "Then you two go for your walk. We'll have dessert when you return."

"Oh, what a lovely idea," Melody said, suddenly full of joy. "What do you think, Mr Williams?"

He wiped his mouth with the napkin again, then stood. "Excellent idea. Let me help you into your coat."

Mrs Grogan nodded. "Look after her, Mr Williams."

He stared at the older woman. "Of course." He looked hurt. It was as though he'd been accused of something he hadn't done. "I would never let anything happen to Miss Harken."

When they were both rugged up, Mrs Grogan gave Melody a basket to bring back her finds. They left the cozy house and headed toward the woods, where Melody had wanted to go.

She hooked her arm through his and it felt as though they were a couple. But of course they weren't.

"It's not terribly far," he said, stealing a glance at her. "This area was mostly cleared when the town was built, but we felt it beneficial to keep the woods intact."

"How long ago was that?"

She pulled her hat a little further down on her head. It was quite chilly out here.

"A little over two years ago. Everyone who lives here came on the wagon train."

She had no idea. No one had told her, but there was no reason they should. "That must have been exciting," she said.

"Yes and no," he said sadly.

She stared at him and hoped he'd tell her what was bothering him.

"Well here we are," he announced, spreading his hands wide. "We're at the edge of the woods. I don't recommend we go in too deep. It's easy to get lost."

"It's beautiful here," she said, running around and picking up pinecones and pine branches for her Christmas decorations.

She couldn't help but grin. "Now all I need is some red and gold ribbon. I wonder if the Mercantile sells ribbon?"

"They do. But I thought you didn't have any money."

Her happiness suddenly disappeared. "You're right. For a minute there, I'd forgotten the terrible situation I'm in."

She shrugged and began to offload her findings. He reached out and stopped her. "Don't do that. We'll work something out, I'm sure," he told her, his fingers intertwining with hers.

He was so close to her face, and if she didn't know better, would have thought he was about to kiss her.

He suddenly pulled back. "If you have everything you need, I suggest we return. It's only going to get colder."

He pulled out his pocket-watch. "Mrs Grogan will be watching the time for sure."

She finished returning all the goodies to the basket and they began their journey back. "It might be cold, but I'm enjoying our stroll," she told him.

He stared into her eyes. "Me too. I enjoy your company, Miss Harken. Very much so."

Her heart fluttered. He didn't say he enjoyed her cooking, which is what he usually said. He had clearly said he enjoyed her company.

"And I enjoy your company, Mr Williams."

They returned via a different route, Mr Williams wanting to show her more of the township. "Oh look," she said, pointing to a little cabin on a hillside. "There's smoke coming out of the chimney. I'll bet it's cozy and warm in there."

He grinned at her. "That's old Mrs Jones place. She only visits town when she needs supplies – about once a month."

"Surely she didn't come on the wagon train alone?" The way Melody understood it, that wouldn't be allowed.

Mr Williams glanced toward the cabin. "Her husband died last year. His was the second funeral this town has seen."

His face went ashen and she knew something was very wrong, but perhaps now was not the time to ask.

He adjusted his scarf around his neck, then tightened his grip on her arm. "We must go quickly. The wind has picked up."

They resumed their trek and Melody suddenly stopped. "Is that..." She touched her nose. "Yes, it's snow!" she said excitedly.

It was only light, and it melted almost the moment it touched the ground, but it truly was snow.

"Oh dear. We must get back quickly. It can be dangerous if the snow gets too heavy. We don't want to be stuck out here."

She looked back toward the woods and watched mesmerized as the snow balanced on the edge of the branches. She'd never seen anything like it.

By the time they arrived back at the edge of town, it was snowing quite heavily. Melody dropped the basket to the ground outside the Grogan's house, then spun around in a circle, watching the snow fall.

"This is magical," she shouted, holding her hands out so the snow would fall into them.

He laughed. "Give it a few weeks and you might change your mind." He didn't laugh often, but when he did, it lit up his face. It was almost like he was a different person. "We'd better get inside. Mrs Grogan will be worrying about you. Because of the snow, I mean."

She nodded and picked up the basket. "We have apple and rhubarb pie waiting. That will help warm us up."

As they made their way toward the gate, she lost her footing and involuntarily screamed. Mr Williams reached out and stopped her landing on the snow-covered ground.

His face was so close to hers, and his strong arms supported her. He stared into her eyes, and lowered his face to hers. "Miss Harken," he said softly, and she was certain this time he would kiss her. Or perhaps that was just wishful thinking?

"Mr Williams," Mrs Grogan said sternly. "What are you doing to Miss Harken?"

He straighten up and pulled Melody with him. "I..."

"I slipped, Mrs Grogan," Melody interrupted. "Mr Williams saved me from falling."

"Hmph!" Mrs Grogan turned and walked inside. "Hurry up then, the pie is getting cold," she said over her shoulder.

Their eyes met, and Melody could see his disappointment. It was nothing compared to hers.

What just happened?

Pete looked down into the bowl containing a huge piece of warm apple and rhubarb pie with cream. A mug of coffee sat in front of him.

He dared not look up with Melody sitting opposite. He didn't know what he'd do if he saw pleading in her eyes. Not that he expected to. They barely knew each other.

What happened outside was an accident. She almost fell, and he stopped her before she hit the ground.

That was it. End of story. At least that's what he tried to convince himself.

"Thank you for saving me, Mr Williams," she said quietly. "I could have been severely injured if you hadn't caught me in time."

He inwardly winced. Now he had no choice but to look at her. "I really didn't do much. I did what any decent person would do – I stopped you from falling."

She studied him. "Now I understand what you meant when you said snow is dangerous."

Mrs Grogan snorted. "Dangerous? Really Mr Williams!" He turned to look at her - she'd obviously never slipped on the stuff.

"You weren't there, Mrs Grogan," Melody chimed in. "If it wasn't for Mr Williams, I would have been flat on my back."

The older woman looked shocked.

"I did tell you Mr Williams saved me. I wasn't lying." She looked hurt to think Mrs Grogan would think she'd tell a lie.

"She could have hit her head and seriously injured herself." He had no idea why he was defending Melody against such insinuations, but he felt it was his duty to do so.

Mrs Grogan looked from one to the other of them. "I believe you. Don't worry yourselves." Then she smiled. "More pie, Mr Williams?"

"I'd love it, but my belly is bursting at the seams. Thank you all for such a wonderful day." He looked directly at Melody as he said the words. The others blended into the background.

Melody got to her feet. "You're not leaving us are you? There's a roaring fire in the sitting room." She refilled the kettle and collected his empty bowl and mug. "I'll get you a fresh coffee."

"If you insist," he said, noting the pleading in her eyes. He certainly enjoyed her company, but didn't want to outstay his welcome. "I don't want to make a nuisance of myself."

"You're never a nuisance, Mr Williams," Mrs Grogan said sternly. "Our door is always open." She smiled then helped Melody clear the rest of the dishes away.

The two men made their way into the sitting room, and chatted about nothing for awhile. It wasn't long before they both dozed in the warmth of the fire. It was funny how the fire in here warmed the house so completely, yet at home, it did little.

Perhaps it was the company that made the difference? He began to doze again, this time lulled into a much deeper sleep, but was awoken with a start.

"Oh, I didn't mean to wake you, Mr Williams," Melody said, placing the hot mug on a small nearby table.

He could get used to this. Spending his day off sitting by the fire after a nice roast and a walk with his wife. Coffee by the fire, and even dozing in his chair.

Was that what Doc Grogan did? He glanced across to see the older man doing just that. He looked so peaceful, and Pete smiled.

He definitely could get used to that.

"Melody," he said quietly, lifting the mug. "I'm very sorry for what happened when you arrived in town."

She put up her hand to stop him. "No need. All is forgiven." She smiled but he wasn't certain the smile was genuine. He needed to find a way to put this right.

Sitting herself down in the empty chair next to him, Melody turned toward him. "I really enjoyed our stroll today. Even if I did embarrass myself toward the end." She looked down into her lap.

He reached across and lifted her chin, then stared into those beautiful eyes. He could easily get lost in them. "Don't feel embarrassed on my account. New snow can be slippery, as you've discovered, and you're not used to it."

He reached out and covered her hand with his own. It felt nice. Her skin was so soft and gentle. She didn't attempt to pull away, and he left it right where it was.

A man could certainly get used to this.

Chapter Seven

Pete hung the sign on the Post Office window: *Back in 15 minutes*

He straightened his tie, did up his jacket, and placed his hat on his head. He snatched up the telegram, and pulled on his thick woolen coat.

Now the snow had arrived, it would be colder than ever. He dragged on his gloves after he locked the door.

He'd intended to visit the Mercantile today, but the telegram brought that visit forward. "Good morning, Edward," he said, handing over the telegram. "This just arrived."

Edward finished with his customer before reading the telegram. "Good. My delivery will finally arrive today. Excellent news. Thank you, Pete."

Pete stayed where he was.

"Is there something else I can help you with?"

Pete looked around the store, ensuring no one could overhear him. "I need some red and gold ribbon," he said quietly.

Edward grinned. "Making something special, are we?" he joked.

It wasn't appreciated. Pete straightenec his shoulders and glared at the Mercantile owner. "It's a gift for a young lady." His patience was running out. "So do you have any? Oh, and some twine too please."

Edward strolled toward a shelf at the back of the store. He handed over a roll of twine. Then he looked thoughtful. "I'm sure I have some ribbon here. It's so long since I've sold any, I can't quite think where it is."

He slowly turned, looking over all the shelves. "Ah! There it is." He stepped toward a shelf of Christmas supplies. "I sell it by the yard or on the roll. Your choice."

"I'll take a roll of each, thank you," he said. His purchases were added to a brown paper bag, and added to his account.

He left the store whistling, and almost skipped as he returned to the Post Office. He hoped his surprise brightened Melody's day. She deserved some happiness.

The rest of the morning went slowly by, but would soon pick up when the train arrived. Once the letters and packages were in, he'd be busy sorting.

This afternoon the Post Office would be overwhelmed with people coming to collect their mail. Those living out of town only came every couple of weeks to collect their mail.

He spent most of the morning tidying up, readying the shelves for the incoming mail.

"Good morning, Mr Williams," she said with a grin.

His head shot up. He was shocked to see Melody standing in front of him. "Good morning. I didn't hear you come in."

She laughed and the tinkling sound made his heart skip a beat. "Mrs Grogan wanted me to ensure you came for luncheon today."

He stared at her. "I couldn't. You've all been too kind, but it can't go on forever."

Her smile dropped, and she suddenly looked saddened. "We enjoy your company," she said. "And it's no sacrifice to have one extra person.

We're having chicken and vegetable soup with biscuits."

It made his mouth water just thinking about it. "It sounds delicious, but I couldn't."

She reached across the counter and snatched up his hands. "Please, Mr Williams," she said quietly. "I do so enjoy your company, and I've made plenty."

He looked into her eyes, and felt drawn in. "How can I say no to that?" He pulled one of her hands to his lips. "I would be very grateful, thank you, Miss Harken. Can you give me a moment? There's something I have to do first."

She nodded and he ran into the residence, returning with the brown paper bag. He'd intended to visit after the Post Office closed, but this would do nicely.

On his return, he put on his coat, slipping the bag into one of the pockets, and was glad to see Melody wore her coat too.

"Did you notice the snow, Mr Williams?" she asked. "It's heavier now. I've never had a white Christmas – this is so exciting!"

He finished buttoning his coat, and she slipped her arm into his. He locked the door, and they were soon on their way.

"I did enjoy our walk into the woods yesterday," she said. "I haven't had a chance to do anything with those bits and pieces yet, but I will."

"Miss Harken," he said gently, pulling the paper bag out of his pocket. "I have a small...gift for you."

She suddenly stopped and turned to face him. "A gift for me? You didn't have to do that." She looked embarrassed at the mere thought.

He handed over the package. "It's not much, but I think you'll like it."

She opened it, then looked down inside the bag. "You didn't? Oh my gosh, Mr Williams, I don't know what to say." Her eyes were full of unshed tears, and one escaped.

He lifted his hand to her cheek, and wiped it away with his gloved hand. It seemed like such a personal thing to do, and he suddenly pulled back.

"You are far too kind, Mr Williams," she said, staring at her gift. "I'll repay you somehow."

"No payment needed," he said. "And none will be accepted. You've done so much for me, and I...I have done nothing but cause you distress."

She didn't disagree.

He hooked his arm back through hers, and they continued on their original mission – luncheon at the Grogan's.

He thoroughly enjoyed his little sojourns with Melody on the rare occasion they occurred.

It was obvious they wouldn't be going off into the woods any time soon, not with the heavy snowfalls they were now experiencing.

It had become very clear Christmas was nudging closer and closer.

A while back, he thought he might be married for Christmas. It would have been nice. Waking up on Christmas morning, with his wife by his side.

Decorating their tree together, eating a roast lunch.

Despite those plans going awry, it was a joy to get to know Melody. She was friendly, helpful, full of life, and a great cook. He'd come to really like her.

No, that wasn't true, he'd come to really care for her. Even in the short time they'd known each other.

"Did you hear me, Mr Williams?" Mrs Grogan's voice came crashing through his thoughts.

Melody was grinning, and so was Mr Grogan. "I'm so sorry, Mrs Grogan, I was a thousand miles away."

She put down her spoon and wiped her mouth with a napkin. "I said that was so kind of you. To purchase those lovely ribbons for Miss Harken."

He felt the heat creep up his neck and face. "It was the least I could do to repay her," he said, glancing at Mrs Grogan. "I...I'm very thankful to you all for what you've done for me. I feel like a different person." He looked down into his near empty soup bowl.

Melody mistook his actions. He was trying to hide his emotions, she assumed he was still hungry.

Mrs Grogan reached out and patted his hand. "You're a good man, Mr Williams. It's not hard to want to help you."

Melody placed the refilled bowl in front of him. "It's true," she said quietly. "Look what you did for me – they must have cost a lot, but you bought them for me anyway."

"I was being selfish," he said flippantly. "I want to see what you make."

Melody stared at him from across the table. "I don't believe that. Just accept that we believe you to be kind, and don't make it out to be something else."

He nodded. She was right, but it felt wrong to say so.

"We'll have to start decorating the house soon. What about the Post Office, Mr Williams?" Mrs Grogan stared at him.

"What about the Post Office?"

Mrs Grogan shuffled in her chair. "May we decorate the Post Office for Christmas?"

"I've never done it before." He scratched his head. Why was it suddenly an issue?

"That's settled then. Miss Harken and I will come over in two days and begin decorating."

Melody grinned at him. They both knew he wouldn't win this battle, so he just gave in.

"Miss Harken," Sheriff Doyle said, standing on the Grogan's doorstep. "Would you mind accompanying me to the Sheriff's Office.

Mrs Grogan looked over her shoulder. "What's this about Sheriff? Did you catch that horrid Mr Johnston?"

"We may have, Mrs Grogan, but I need Miss Harken's assistance."

They followed the Sheriff to his office, and the two women sat opposite him. From across the desk he shuffled some papers about.

"I know you've given us a description before, Miss Harken," he said gently. "But can you describe this man again?"

Melody winced. She'd rather forget the whole incident. But she had to do whatever it took to catch him in case he duped some other poor unsuspecting woman. "He was about six foot tall, black hair, and beady brown eyes."

The Sheriff smiled. He opened a folder on his desk, then held up a poster. "Would this be the man?"

Melody gasped. "You got him? You got the two-faced cad? I hope you lock him up for the rest of his life."

She was shaking, and Mrs Grogan put her arms around the younger woman. "Don't upset yourself, Miss Harken." She turned to Sheriff Doyle. "Did you get him? I certainly hope he's locked up in jail now!"

The Sheriff smiled again. "Yes, he is locked up – for now at least. There will be a trial of course, but I needed your confirmation this was the man." He put the wanted poster back into the folder. "You were not his only victim, Miss Harken, but he won't be doing it again for a very long time. There are at least another ten women this man stole from."

She sighed. "Thank goodness you found him."

"Unfortunately, we weren't able to recover any of the money, but at least he's locked up now."

She stood and stared at Sheriff Doyle. "Thank you so much," she said. "You have no idea how happy this makes me."

The two women headed back home. Melody would sleep better tonight.

The two women shuffled around the Post Office as he worked.

It was distracting to say the least. They'd made colorful paper chains and hung them about the room. Next they'd be wanting to decorate his house.

That wasn't about to happen.

All the businesses in Dayton Falls had begun to decorate their shop windows, as well as the insides. He'd never bothered — no one worried whether or not the Post Office was festive. At least they'd never mentioned it if they did.

But it did look good. Cheerful. It made him feel excited for Christmas. He'd not felt that way since...

"What do you think, Mr Williams?" Melody looked across at him expectantly.

He came out from behind the counter and surveyed the room. "I rather like it, I must say." She giggled, and it warmed his heart.

"I have something for you, Mr Williams," she said, reaching into a box.

Mrs Grogan stood back and looked on proudly.

"It's a Christmas wreath – it hangs on the door." She lifted it out and turned it to face him.

It was incredible. He'd never seen anything like it. "It's very beautiful. How on earth you made something so beautiful from all those pine pieces from off the ground, I'll never know."

"They're beautiful because of the ribbons you bought." She didn't give him a chance to answer, instead, went outside and fiddled about until she managed to get the wreath to hang on the door.

He stood behind her and checked it out. "It looks superb sitting there." It really did.

She turned to him and smiled. "Thank you, Mr Williams."

"Call me Pete. Mrs Grogan is the only person in town who calls me Mr Williams."

"Thank you, Peter," she said with a grin.

Pete had his hand on the door handle and was about to open it but paused. "Melody," he said quietly. "Would you come to dinner with me tonight?"

He looked away. He didn't want to see the pity in her eyes when she said no, as she surely would. "We'd go to *Edna's Diner*. It's a little more private than the hotel."

He stole a glance and was surprised when her eyes opened wide in surprise. "Of course I will. Thank you, Mr...Peter!"

She leaned forward and hugged him tight. It felt so good, so right. He wrapped his arms around her, and pulled her a little closer.

He knew he shouldn't, especially with Mrs Grogan nearby, but when he glanced up, he saw the old dear staring at them and grinning.

Melody sat on the bed and took a calming breath.

An invitation to dinner was the last thing she expected from Mr Williams. He didn't seem that sort of man. The dating sort that is.

She glanced across at the open wardrobe. The hardest decision she'd had to make for some time was this one – what to wear.

She wanted to make a good impression, so needed to look her best tonight. One good thing Father had done for her was to ensure she always looked her best. For that she would be forever grateful.

She wavered between the pink gown with gold thread, and the soft blue gown with seed beads sewn into the button-up bodice and hem.

Hearing a knock at the front door, she hurriedly decided on the latter.

She dressed as quickly as she could, then pulled on her best boots, and last of all, chose her favorite hat.

It was a soft velvet hat, that sat back on her head. Mother had bought this particular one because it matched the blue gown almost perfectly. It had pretty blue ribbons to tie under her chin, and was decorated with ostrich feathers, and pale blue silk flowers.

Mother had loved this hat, and it was very special to Melody.

There was a light tap at her door. "Miss Harken, are you ready? Mr Williams is here."

Her heart skipped a beat. She stared at herself in the full-length mirror.

Would he approve?

She straightened her skirt. Not that it needed straightening — she fully recognized her nervousness. It was silly to be anxious. They'd spend plenty of time together over the past weeks.

But not on a date. This was a completely different scenario.

Satisfied, she stepped out of her bedroom, and into the sitting room where she knew he'd be waiting. He stood as she entered the room, nodding acknowledgement of her presence.

Then he froze. He literally stood there staring. His eyes scanned her from top to bottom.

The silence became uncomfortable. *Did he disapprove?*

When he finally found his voice, it was barely above a whisper. "You look beautiful, Miss Harken," he said, emotion clearly overtaking him.

Mrs Grogan handed him Melody's coat, and he helped her into it.

"I, I booked a table at *Edna's Diner*," he said. "Not that she's ever full."

Melody didn't know what to say, so just nodded.

"Have fun," Mrs Grogan said as they left.

Mr Williams looked nervous, and hardly said a word as they walked the short distance to the diner.

"Is everything alright, Mr Williams? You're awfully quiet."

He glanced across at her. "I have a few things on my mind," he said gently.

Her heart beat rapidly. "Perhaps now is not a good time?" She hoped he didn't change his mind, despite her words.

He stared at her. "It's now or never," he muttered. At least that's what it sounded like.

Edna's daughter, Lizzie, met them at the door, and took their coats. The warmth of the roaring fire was a welcome relief from the freezing temperature outside.

She showed them to their table, which wasn't far from the fire. "What do you recommend?" he asked before she had a chance to hand them the menus.

"We have a Christmas menu at the moment," Lizzie said. "Christmas dinner with all the trimmings. Plum pudding with custard for dessert."

He glanced across to Melody and she nodded her agreement. "We'll both have that. Thank you, Lizzie."

Melody watched as Lizzie entered the kitchen where her mother was cooking. She felt his hand slip over hers. It felt nice, and she glanced across at him and smiled.

"You don't mind?"

She shook her head. "Not at all." She slid her other hand over the top of his. It felt good, and she didn't want him to remove it.

The flames from the fire played across his face, and the quiet in the diner made it feel very romantic. She'd never been on a date with a man before, and she wasn't sure what to expect.

Lizzie returned with some sliced bread, which she placed in the center of the table. She also left a good portion of butter for them.

When they were alone again, Mr Williams reached over and held her other hand. "I was wondering, Miss Harken…"

"Some water for you both."

Melody knew Lizzie was being helpful, but it was obvious Mr Williams was trying to tell her something, but was nervous. "Yes, Mr Williams?"

"I was wondering…"

"Here you are," Lizzie said, dropping their plates in front of them.

"Go ahead, Mr Williams," she said quietly.

He quickly let go of her hand. "It can wait until after we've eaten."

She looked at him curiously. He seemed a little agitated tonight. Melody wondered what was on his mind.

"Mmmm, this is nice," she said between mouthfuls.

He looked up at her. "It's not as good as your cooking. I've been spoiled now." He grinned and she felt warmth flood her body.

They finished their main course, and it wasn't long before their plates were cleared away. The puddings arrived soon after.

"Oh my," Melody said. "This is scrumptious."

"That it is."

He plunged his hand into his pocket, then suddenly pulled it out again. Melody had noticed him doing the same thing several times throughout the night, but said nothing. She wondered if it was just nerves.

When they finished eating, he ordered coffee for two. Melody took a sip.

"Miss Harken," he said, glancing across at her. "I feel I need to explain myself."

"Oh?"

"When you arrived – I was very remiss. I had no right to send you away."

"Oh, but you did, Mr Williams. You weren't expecting me." She reached across and touched his hand.

He looked down, and slipped his fingers through hers. "There are things you don't know about me. Things you need to know."

He went on to explain about Priscilla and how she'd lost her life on the wagon train.

"I'm so sorry, Mr Williams. What a terrible thing to endure." She felt so bad for him, but wasn't sure why he was telling her all this.

"I sent you away because I felt guilty. I thought it meant I didn't care for my dear Priscilla anymore, but now I know that's not true.

I've realized she would want me to be happy." He stared into her eyes. This was obviously what had been bothering him.

Melody didn't know what to say, so just nodded.

"Miss Harken," he said, plunging his hand into his pocket again. "Will you forgive me?"

Is that what he wanted? Her forgiveness? "Of course I do. What a silly thing to say."

Lizzie scooped up their empty cups. This was not the place to be if you wanted to talk, that much had become blatantly obvious.

The moment the thought entered her head, Melody felt guilty. Lizzie was just doing her job.

"Miss Harken," Mr Williams said again, only this time much more quietly. He reached into his pocket and pulled out a small velveteen box, then opened it to reveal an engagement ring. "Will you marry me?"

Chapter Eight

Arriving back at the Grogan's, Melody showed the ring to Mrs Grogan. "Mr Williams asked me to marry him," she said happily. "It's a beautiful ring."

Mrs Grogan beamed. "When is the wedding to be?"

"Uh," he was flustered. "We haven't thought that far ahead."

"Sit yourself down, Mr Williams, and we'll have coffee." Mrs Grogan stoked the fire to coax the flames higher, and soon enough the kettle boiled.

She put a mug in front of him, and pulled a tin from the cupboard, placing slices of pound cake on a plate. Pete reached for a slice – his belly was full, but he couldn't resist Melody's cooking.

His fiancé filled the other mugs and they all sat around the table discussing the wedding.

"We don't want to wait too long," he said. "At least I don't. What about you, Miss Harken?"

Mrs Grogan took a sip of her coffee. "For goodness sakes, are you two going to go through life calling each other Mr Williams and Miss Harken?" She looked annoyed.

The young couple looked at each other, then began to laugh. It was true, they were being far more formal than necessary.

He reached across the table and gently took Melody's hand. "Do you think Preacher Brown would agree to Christmas Eve, Mrs Grogan?"

She near choked on her coffee. "Christmas Eve? Are you crazy? That's a little over a week away!"

"I have my wedding gown. Well, my mother's wedding gown. I don't know about Mr...uh, Peter, but I don't want a big fuss."

"That works for me," he said.

Mrs Grogan cleared her throat. "Every bride should have a proper wedding," she said abruptly. "And you, Miss Harken, will have a proper wedding."

Doctor Grogan had said barely a word up to this point. "You go and see Preacher Brown tomorrow, Pete. Book that date."

"I'll organize the Ladies Auxiliary for the reception. Everyone will be happy to pitch in. This is exciting – our first-ever wedding!" Mrs Grogan stood. "And now, Mr Williams, it's time for you to leave. We need to do a fitting for that wedding dress."

He gulped down the last mouthful of his coffee. There was no way Pete was going to argue with Mrs Grogan.

He pulled on his warm coat and wrapped his scarf around his neck. He pulled his hat down over his head and pulled on his gloves.

Melody walked him to the front door to say goodnight. It felt a little cheeky, but he lightly kissed her lips. She gazed at him, and put her fingers to her lips.

His still tingled when he arrived home.

He lit the fire in his sitting room. The house felt so cold; it had never bothered him before.

Before Miss Melody Harken that was.

Before his life meant something again.

Before he thought there was even a smidgeon of hope that he'd feel happiness ever again in his life.

He was marrying the woman he'd once rejected. Back then, he didn't know her. But now he did. Now he had a whole new perspective of the alluring Miss Harken. Melody.

His soon-to-be wife. The woman he loved.

Melody stood at the back of the Dayton Falls church, her arm hooked through that of her surrogate father, Doctor Henry Grogan.

In the short time she'd known him, Doc Grogan had become like a father to her, and when he'd offered to walk her down the aisle, she'd cried. Her own father should have been there to do that, but sadly he wasn't.

He stood proudly next to her, in his Sunday best suit, talking quietly, trying to calm her. Not that she was terribly nervous; she was ready to marry Peter Williams. He'd turned out to be such a kind and gentle man, despite her first impression of him.

She wore the dress her mother had worn for her wedding, and apart from a hem adjustment, it fitted just fine.

The one thing she didn't have was a veil to wear with her dress. Mother's had been lost when they moved to Westlake for her father to take up his post as doctor there.

When she mentioned it to Mrs Grogan, the older woman quietly left the room, and returned with a hat box. "It's not perfect," she'd said. "But it's better than nothing."

She pulled out an aged wedding veil. Once pure white, it was now off-white in color, but still in pristine condition. It had been well preserved.

It had an off-white band, with a piece of off-white velvet strewn across it. A small ruffle of tulle held two imperfect white feathers, and there were small gems scattered on each side.

"I couldn't," Melody said, staring at the piece of beauty before her.

Mrs Grogan patted her hand. "I would be honored if you would, my dear."

Melody reached up to ensure the headpiece sat firmly on her head, and it did. As she looked down the aisle, she saw Peter standing there, gazing at her, waiting for her arrival.

The church held as many parishioners as it had on Sunday. This being the town's first wedding it had been a big attraction. At least that's what she'd been told.

Mrs Jensen from the Ladies Auxiliary sat at the organ, and began to play the Wedding March. She looked across at Doc Grogan who patted her hand. "Ready?" he whispered.

With no children of their own, this would be the only opportunity he'd have to walk a bride down the aisle. Melody was happy she would be that bride.

The town had been a flutter with not only Christmas organization, but preparations for the wedding. Peter had been adamant they'd marry Christmas Eve. She wasn't quite sure why.

Her heart did a little dance as she was delivered to her groom, and when he took her hand, warmth spread through her body.

Despite her age, despite the circumstances of their meeting, Melody knew this man, Peter Williams, was her forever man.

"I love you, Melody," he said softly, then leaned in and kissed her cheek. His eyes sparkled, and his smile set her heart alight.

"I love you too, Peter," she said, fighting back tears of joy.

"We are gathered here today…"

The reception was a huge success.

The Ladies Auxiliary had been more than a little excited to be catering for the town's first wedding, and they'd ensured it was spectacular.

As she looked around, Melody couldn't believe the array of food available. She sat next to Peter at the bridal table, with the Grogan's by their side.

They'd become like parents to them both, and the four were all very close now.

Melody had decided to bake the wedding cake, despite the protests from Mrs Grogan. "A bride should never have to bake her own wedding cake," she'd said. But Melody didn't mind.

It wasn't every day you got married. Besides, there was no one else in town who could do it. She'd carefully decorated it, and was more than a little pleased with the results.

It now stood proudly on the bridal table, and soon she would get to cut the cake with her husband. She fought back a sob.

Two months ago she was living in Westlake, with not a care in the world. So much had happened in that time. She'd lost her father, her home, and had met the most wonderful man.

Now she was looking forward to what life as Mrs Peter Williams would bring.

Doc Grogan stood up, and tapped on his glass to quieten down their guests. "I'd like to propose a toast to the newlyweds," he said, and lifted his glass to his lips.

This was the most animated Melody had ever seen him. He didn't often have much to say, except to his patients.

"To the newly weds," everyone repeated.

After the doc had sat down again, Peter stood, his glass in hand. "Less than two months ago, I was living a very lonely life," he said, gazing down at her. "I'd never set eyes on this beauty. Then one day she came into my life, and everything changed."

He reached down and took her hand. "But I was a cad, and rejected her at first," he said. "I'm not sorry for that," he added, and Melody heard the gasps from their guests.

"I'm not sorry because it meant I got to know her better, and I'm so glad that I did." He lifted her hand to his lips and kissed it. "I got to know what a kind and gentle soul she was. We spent time together, we learned to love each other.

I'd like to thank the Grogan's for all their help, especially Mrs Grogan for her devious plan to get us together." Everyone laughed, even Mrs

Grogan. "Oh, and I'd like to add, my wife is an amazing cook."

He smiled down at her, and Melody realized she'd never been so happy in her life. "To my beautiful wife." He lifted the glass and took a sip.

"To Melody," the guests said in unison.

With the formalities over, everyone was left to enjoy the food. Peter and Melody wandered around, talking to the guests. It gave her an opportunity to get to know people better. She knew she was going to love living in this outback town called Dayton Falls. But most of all, she knew she was going love getting to know her husband better.

They arrived home later that afternoon, after all the celebrations were over. They stood on the doorstep to the residence, and Peter unlocked the door.

She didn't know this entrance existed, as he rarely used it. The Post Office had been his life before, now he vowed to make Melody his priority, with his work coming a deservedly second-best.

He looked across at her, resplendent in her wedding dress. He looked her up and down. What did he do to deserve such a wonderful wife?

He leaned in and cupped her cheeks with his hands, and kissed her gently. She leaned into his shoulder, and rested her head. He wrapped his arms around his new bride, and sighed.

He could stand like this forever, but that would never do. They had more important things to do.

Dropping his hands, she straightened up and stared into his eyes. He stole another kiss, then scooped her up and carried her across the threshold to his home.

Their home.

He truly loved this woman, and wanted nothing more than to spend time with her – for the rest of their lives.

Epilogue

Twelve months later

Peter paced the room.

He was fully aware of the consequences of child birth, having already lost one wife that way.

Each scream saw him wincing and covering his ears. "How much longer, Mrs Grogan?" he asked as the older woman came out to give him an update.

"That I cannot tell you," she said gently. "But she is doing fine. I don't think it will be long and you'll be a father."

A father. Him, a father. That sounded good.

Another scream, this one prolonged. "I'm not sure I can take much more of this," he said. "Knowing that my dear Melody is in so much pair."

He blinked back the tears that had threatened to push through for several hours.

Mrs Grogan led him to an armchair. "Sit yourself down and don't worry. Henry will keep her safe." She disappeared into the kitchen and came back a short time later with a mug of coffee. "It won't help much, but will soothe your nerves."

"Thanks."

Doc Grogan came out of the bedroom as he took the last gulp of coffee. It had helped – just a little – and he felt a little calmer. The lessening screams had helped too.

The doc approached him, and shook his hand.

"You have a beautiful baby girl," he said, tears glistening in his eyes. This child would be like a grandchild to him.

"I have a daughter? I have a daughter!" he said, rushing to his wife and child.

Pete sat on the side of the bed, and leaned into his exhausted wife. "Thank you," he said quietly. "Thank you for everything. For my beautiful daughter," he glanced across at the baby, wrapped up tightly, and in her mother's arms. "She is the best Christmas gift I've ever received."

THE END

From the Author

Thank you so much for reading my book – I hope you enjoyed it.

I would greatly appreciate you leaving a review on Amazon, even if it is only a one-liner. It helps to have my books more visible on Amazon!

If you would like to read more books based in the outback town of Dayton Falls, check out my historical series, Mail Order Brides of Dayton Falls.

You might also enjoy reading other books in the Spinster Mail-Order Brides:

Bonus Book – A Shadowed Groom for Christmas – Marisa Masterson

Book 1 - A Marshal for Christmas - P. Creeden

Book 3 - A Husband for Christmas - Margaret Tanner

Book 4 - A Farmer for Christmas- Marisa Masterson

Book 5 - A Family for Christmas - Cheryl Wright